I NEED A LUNCH BOX

by Jeannette Caines   pictures by Pat Cummings

SCHOLASTIC INC.
New York Toronto London Auckland Sydney

Text copyright © 1988 by Jeannette Franklin Caines.
Illustrations copyright © 1988 by Pat Cummings.
All rights reserved. Published by Scholastic Inc.,
730 Broadway, New York, NY 10003,
by arrangement with HarperCollins Children's Books.
Printed in the U.S.A.
Typography by Bettina Rossner.
ISBN 0-590-47262-3

3 4 5 6 7 8 9 10   23   99 98 97 96

For Matthew Lowenbraun, who gave me the idea,
Gwen Meyers, who loved it,
and
Lina Goodhue, who bought my Abby her first lunch box.
J.F.C.

For Percidia
P.C.

My sister Doris got a brand new lunch box.
I need a lunch box too.
But Mommy said no lunch box until I start
school.

Last week Daddy bought us new shoes.
Brown school shoes for Doris.
Black sneakers with yellow laces for me.

We walked past the lunch box counter, twice.
I need a lunch box!

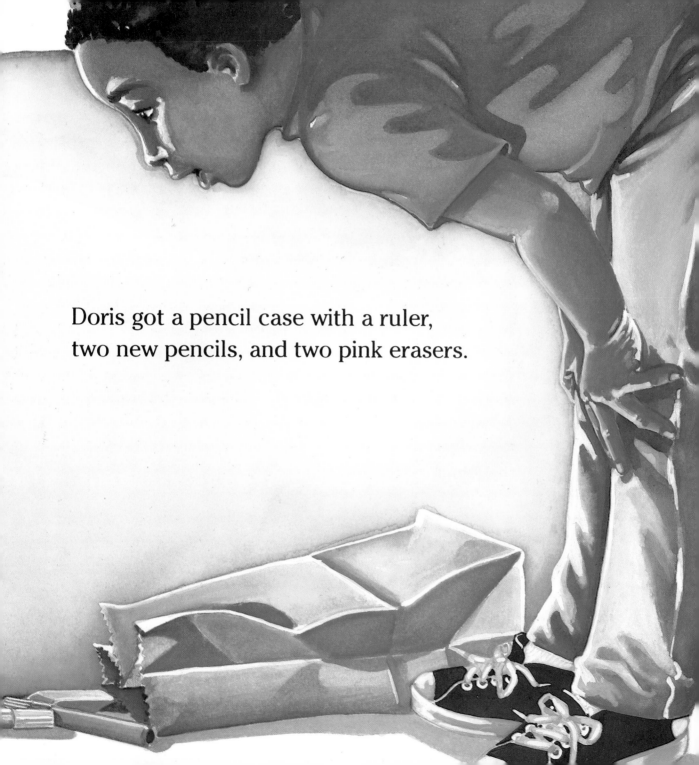

Doris got a pencil case with a ruler,
two new pencils, and two pink erasers.

All I got was a coloring book about space men and a box of crayons— but no lunch box.

Yesterday Doris got book covers, a raincoat, and an umbrella—all because she's going to first grade.

If I had a lunch box I could keep
my crayons in it. Or my marbles,
or bug collection, or toy animals.

I dreamed I had five lunch boxes, one for every day.
Blue for Monday…

TUESDAY

Green for Tuesday...

Red for Wednesday...

Yellow for Friday.

I filled them with peanut butter and jelly sandwiches, apples, oranges, chocolate cake, cookies and pies and donuts.
And then we had a lunch box parade.

Doris starts school today.
I felt sorta bad when Mommy handed Doris
her brand new lunch box.
But then Daddy said, "I have a surprise for you."

Wow!
I got a lunch box too!